Published by Delacorte Press
Bantam Doubleday Dell Publishing Group, Inc.
666 Fifth Avenue, New York, New York 10103

This edition was first published in Great Britain by Walker Books Ltd.

Copyright © 1989 Ron Maris

The trademark Delacorte ᴿ is registered in the U.S. Patent
and Trademark Office.

Library of Congress Cataloging-in-Publication Data
Maris, Ron.
Bernard's boring day / Ron Maris.   p.   cm.
Summary: Bernard the garden gnome sits fishing quietly by the
pool, totally unaware of the animals' activity around him, which the
reader sees by lifting flaps.
ISBN 0-385-29948-6
1. Toy and movable books – Specimens. [1. Gnomes – Fiction.
2. Fishing – Fiction. 3. Animals – Fiction. 4. Toy and movable
books.] I. Title.
PZ7.B338975Bd 1990                                    89.31716
[E] – dc 19                                               CIP
                                                          AC

Manufactured in Italy
First U.S.A. printing March 1990
10  9  8  7  6  5  4  3  2  1

# Bernard's
# Boring Day

## Ron Maris

Delacorte
Press

Bernard is sitting quietly

Everything is calm,

and thinking.

everything is peaceful.

Nothing ever happens...

Bernard is still sitting
quietly by the pool.

Everything is calm,

Nothing
ever happens...

by the pool.